Dear Parent:
Your child's love of reading starts here!

Every child learns to read in a different way and at his or her own speed. Some go back and forth between reading levels and read favorite books again and again. Others read through each level in order. You can help your young reader improve and become more confident by encouraging his or her own interests and abilities. From books your child reads with you to the first books he or she reads alone, there are I Can Read Books for every stage of reading:

SHARED READING
Basic language, word repetition, and whimsical illustrations, ideal for sharing with your emergent reader

BEGINNING READING
Short sentences, familiar words, and simple concepts for children eager to read on their own

READING WITH HELP
Engaging stories, longer sentences, and language play for developing readers

READING ALONE
Complex plots, challenging vocabulary, and high-interest topics for the independent reader

I Can Read Books have introduced children to the joy of reading since 1957. Featuring award-winning authors and illustrators and a fabulous cast of beloved characters, I Can Read Books set the standard for beginning readers.

A lifetime of discovery begins with the magical words **"I Can Read!"**

Visit www.icanread.com for information on enriching your child's reading experience.

HarperCollins Children's Books,
a division of HarperCollins Publishers,
195 Broadway, New York, NY 10007

HarperCollins Publishers,
Macken House, 39/40 Mayor Street Upper,
Dublin 1, D01 C9W8, Ireland

I Can Read® and I Can Read Book® are trademarks of HarperCollins Publishers.

Clydeo versus Peanut Butter
Copyright © 2025 by Invisible Universe Inc.
All rights reserved. Manufactured in Johor, Malaysia.
No part of this book may be used or reproduced in any manner whatsoever without written permission except in the case of brief quotations embodied in critical articles and reviews. Without limiting the exclusive rights of any author, contributor, or the publisher of this publication, any unauthorized use of this publication to train generative artificial intelligence (AI) technologies is expressly prohibited. HarperCollins also exercises their rights under Article 4(3) of the Digital Single Market Directive 2019/790 and expressly reserves this publication from the text and data mining exception.
harpercollins.com

ISBN 978-0-06-337240-5 (pbk.) — ISBN 978-0-06-337241-2

Book design by Rick Farley

25 26 27 28 29 PCA 10 9 8 7 6 5 4 3 2 1   First Edition

Clydeo
versus Peanut Butter

by Jennifer Aniston
illustrated by Bruno Jacob

HARPER

An Imprint of HarperCollinsPublishers

Clydeo's family wanted treats. "Will you make peanut butter cookies?" his uncle asked.

Clydeo loved his family, and he loved to bake.

"Just you wait," he said.

"I'll make the best cookies ever!"

Clydeo had never made peanut butter cookies before. "Maybe I should taste the peanut butter first," he said.

He took a big spoonful.

The peanut butter was super sticky!

Clydeo tried and tried,
but he couldn't open his mouth.
He couldn't even speak.

"What's wrong?" asked Clydeo's dad.

Clydeo grunted.

"Cat got your tongue?" said his dad.

Clydeo shook his head.

Clydeo went to his uncle.

He tried acting out his problem.

"Are we playing charades?" his uncle asked. "How many words?"

Next, Clydeo found his cousin.

He tried drawing what happened.

"Nice picture," she said.

"Is that a funky chicken?"

Then, Clydeo ran to his grandma.

He grunted and pointed at his mouth.

"You're hungry?" she said.

"Me too.

I can't wait for those cookies."

Clydeo wrote down what happened.

"What does it say?"

asked his second cousin.

"I can't read your handwriting."

Clydeo was sad.

Nobody understood him.

At last, Clydeo found his mother in the kitchen.

He pointed at the peanut butter.

He pointed at his mouth.

He tried to talk.

"Is your mouth glued shut?" asked Clydeo's mom.

Clydeo nodded over and over.

Finally, someone understood!

But could she help him?

"Have you tried drinking milk?" asked Clydeo's mom.

Clydeo tried.

His mouth stayed shut.

Then his mom

had a smart idea.

Why not use a straw?

Finally, Clydeo's mouth opened.

"I can talk again!" he cried.

But his family only wanted to know one thing: "Where are our peanut butter cookies?"

"Forget peanut butter," said Clydeo. "This time, it's sugar cookies!"

And they were SO yummy!